74. Miw

I Can Read!

SHARED

My First READING

Biscuit
Finds a Friend

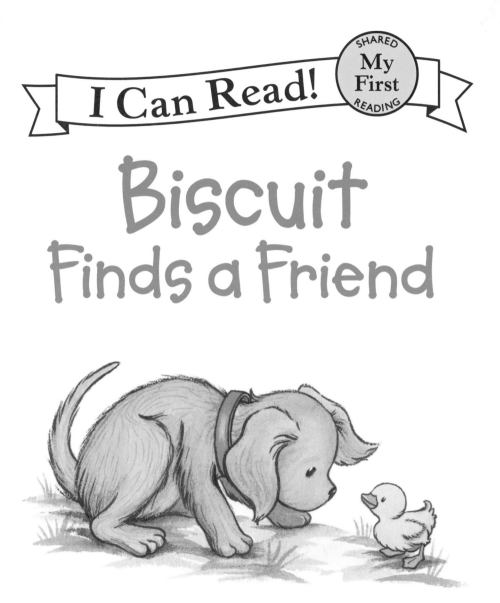

story by ALYSSA SATIN CAPUCILLI
pictures by PAT SCHORIES

HarperCollins*Publishers*

HarperCollins®, 🐾®, and I Can Read Book® are trademarks of HarperCollins Publishers Inc.

Biscuit Finds a Friend Text copyright © 1997 by Alyssa Satin Capucilli Illustrations copyright © 1997 by Pat Schories All rights reserved.
Manufactured in China. For information address HarperCollins Children's Books, a division of HarperCollins Publishers, 10 East 53rd Street, New York, NY 10022.
www.harperchildrens.com
Library of Congress Cataloging-in-Publication Data
Capucilli, Alyssa.
   Biscuit finds a friend / story by Alyssa Satin Capucilli ; pictures by Pat Schories.
      p.   cm. — (A my first I can read book)
   Summary: A puppy helps a little duck find its way home to the pond.
   ISBN-10: 0-06-027412-3 (trade bdg.) — ISBN-13: 978-0-06-027412-2 (trade bdg.)
   ISBN-10: 0-06-027413-1 (lib. bdg.) — ISBN-13: 978-0-06-027413-9 (lib. bdg.)
   ISBN-10: 0-06-444243-8 (pbk.) — ISBN-13: 978-0-06-444243-5 (pbk.)
      [1. Dogs—Fiction. 2. Ducks—Fiction.] I. Schories, Pat, ill. II. Title. III. Series.
PZ7.C179Bis 1997   96-18368
[E]—dc20   CIP
                                                                                                  AC

10 11 12 13 SCP 20 19 18 17 16 15 14
❖

For two very special friends,
Margaret Jean O'Connor and Willie Hornick.

Woof! Woof!

What has Biscuit found?

Is it a ball?

Woof!

Is it a bone?

Woof!

Quack!

It is a little duck.

The little duck is lost.

Woof! Woof!

We will bring
the little duck
back to the pond.

Woof! Woof!

Here, little duck.
Here is the pond.

Here are your mother
and your father.
Quack!

Here are your brothers
and your sisters.
Quack! Quack!

The ducks say thank you.
Thank you for finding
the little duck.

Quack!
The little duck
wants to play.

Quack!
Woof!

Quack!
Woof!

Splash!

Biscuit fell into the pond!

Silly Biscuit.

You are all wet!

Woof!
Oh no, Biscuit.
Not a big shake!

Woof!

Time to go home, Biscuit.

Quack! Quack!

Say good-bye, Biscuit.

Woof! Woof!

Good-bye, little duck.

Biscuit has found
a new friend.